I0607798

Out of Time

PRAISE FOR *STORYSHARES*

"One of the brightest innovators and game-changers in the education industry."
– Forbes

"Your success in applying research-validated practices to promote literacy serves as a valuable model for other organizations seeking to create evidence-based literacy programs."

- Library of Congress

"We need powerful social and educational innovation, and Storyshares is breaking new ground. The organization addresses critical problems facing our students and teachers. I am excited about the strategies it brings to the collective work of making sure every student has an equal chance in life."
– Teach For America

"Around the world, this is one of the up-and-coming trailblazers changing the landscape of literacy and education."
- International Literacy Association

"It's the perfect idea. There's really nothing like this. I mean wow, this will be a wonderful experience for young people."   - Andrea Davis Pinkney, Executive Director, Scholastic

"Reading for meaning opens opportunities for a lifetime of learning. Providing emerging readers with engaging texts that are designed to offer both challenges and support for each individual will improve their lives for years to come. Storyshares is a wonderful start."
- David Rose, Co-founder of CAST & UDL

Out of Time

Vivian Wolkoff

STORYSHARES

Story Share, Inc.
New York. Boston. Philadelphia

Copyright © 2022 by Vivian Wolkoff

All rights reserved.

Published in the United States by Story Share, Inc.

The characters and events in this book are fictitious. Any similarity to real persons, living or dead, is entirely coincidental.

Storyshares

Story Share, Inc.

24 N. Bryn Mawr Avenue #340

Bryn Mawr, PA 19010-3304

www.storyshares.org

Inspiring reading with a new kind of book.

Interest Level: High School

Grade Level Equivalent: 3.8

9781642614725

Book design by Storyshares

Printed in the United States of America

Storyshares Presents

1

"It's just a party," Emmett said. "Please, Mom. Camila will be there. Can I go?"

Mom sighed and shook her head a little, a small smile on her lips. She never could say no to Emmett. "Be home by eleven."

Emmett kissed her cheek and rushed out the door. He had been waiting for Mom to come home from work. He was already dressed up, dying to ask her for permission. He was so desperate to go that he forgot his pad on the table, a sketch half finished. As he stepped out of their rundown building, Emmett paused. He smiled at the night sky, his whole life stretching ahead of him.

The night was full of possibilities. *He* was full of possibilities.

2

He would go to the party at Malik's place and laugh with his friends, cracking jokes. Their voices would rise above the music. He would spot Camila from across the room, his stomach clenching in excitement and nerves as she smiled. He would take one small step at a time towards her and her girlfriends. He would lick his dry lips and ask her if she wanted to get a drink with him, desperately trying to play it cool and failing miserably. His heart would soar when she said yes, her eyes shining and her full lips curling into a smile. By the end of the night, after spending hours talking to her, Emmett would kiss Camila for the first time.

Emmett continued to fantasize about his life ahead...

3

In the coming year, he would be just an ordinary kid. He would keep on sketching. He would start dating Camila. He would go to school and hang out with his friends. He would help Mom around the house and look after his baby sister when Mom had to work late. He would listen to music. He would go to the movies.

There would always be that itch, though: the need to create and to understand the world through art. When graduation came, Emmett would do the unthinkable. He would turn down a scholarship and the chance to go to college so he could focus on his art. Everyone would think he was crazy...including himself. Only Mom would support him.

"I don't understand what you're doing," Mom would say. "But if that's what your heart wants, then I'm by your side. Always."

It would take years for Emmett to understand what those words meant to him. It would take him even longer to thank Mom.

4

In the years after high school, maybe Camila would break up with Emmet. She would give him plenty of excuses. Maybe they wanted different things. She would want to become a doctor and he would want to become an artist. She wouldn't say it, but Emmett would know that none of those were the real reason she'd leave him. Her family didn't see their relationship with kind eyes, old prejudices working against Emmett even though he did his best to fight the biases. Without Camila, he would move across the country, with little money and no plan.

Emmett would get a job and work on his art, taking classes here and there. He would fall in and out of love. He would make beautiful things and have his mind challenged. He would find his message and how he could share it. Suddenly, after years of struggle and learning and stretching himself to his limit, Emmett's art would catch fire. He would go viral. He'd go from broke to rich in a handful of years.

5

Perhaps, on one quiet night when he went home for the holidays, Emmett would run into Camila. She would have become a doctor, a surgeon. She would have moved to the same city that Emmett had moved to. She would apologize for the way things ended, and Emmett would realize that it had been for the best. He would tell her that. He would offer to buy her a beer at a nearby bar. To his shock, she would agree.

Talking to Camila would feel like going home. They would have a great time and Camila would, half-jokingly, suggest they meet again once they returned to their lives in the city. She would believe that someone as rich and famous as Emmett, who would have dated models and become friends with NBA stars, would never hang out with her. To her shock, Emmett would take her up on the offer.

In no time, they would fall for each other all over again. After five years of dating, Emmett would ask her to marry him. Camila would say yes. They would get married in the spring and, the following winter, Camila would tell him that Emmett would be a dad. With his son in his arms, Emmett would look up and smile at the night sky. Life would be full of possibilities. His son would be full of possibilities.

But those possibilities were just that...possibilities.

6

Tonight, Emmett had a party to go to.

He let out another sigh and climbed the handful of steps that connected building to street. He cupped his hands in front of his mouth and blew, tasting his breath. Emmett frowned. He should not have had the garlic bread. He looked over his shoulder. He had gum in his backpack. He could go back inside and-

A hard shove pushed Emmett to the floor. Two white kids ran past him, both looking over their shoulders. One of them was tucking something in the waistband of his jeans. The other was laughing. Neither of them spared Emmett another glance. Still, Emmett shrank and looked away. He had lived in that area long enough to know that he should look the other way when someone carrying a gun ran past him.

He picked himself up and dusted off his pants, walking along. Malik's house was at the end of the block, but it was still early. Emmett thought he had time to pop by the convenience store and get some gum. Besides, it would be good to just let those two white kids keep running and put some more distance between him and them. His mother would be proud of him when he told her later. She had always told him to avoid people like those kids.

He was about to cross the street when he saw the lights. Red and blue and pale. Two officers, their uniforms as dark as the night sky, were talking to the woman at the convenience store. Her face was pale, and she had a nasty gash on her forehead. She was raising an ice pack to her head when her eyes landed on Emmett. Her bottom lip trembled, and her eyes filled with tears. She pointed a shaky finger his way.

7

Emmett froze, his eyes huge on his face. His heartbeat was frantic. One look at him and the cops would see nothing but his dark skin. Nothing but someone who was up to no good. His feet stumbled back. One step. Two steps. As the cops turned to him, Emmett shoved his hand in his pocket. He could call his mom. She could come here and explain everything. She could help him.

Everything happened too fast to stop and too slow to ignore.

The younger cop, his face red and his words full of anger, raised his gun. The other one told Emmett to drop it...whatever *it* was. Emmett pulled his hand from his pocket, cell phone clutched between his fingers. He could explain. He had done nothing wrong.

Shots.

The cell phone fell to the floor. Emmett looked down at his belly, where pain speared him from his gut. There was so much red. He tumbled as the cops continued to scream at him. Emmett covered the holes in his stomach with his hands, trying to keep it all inside. He blinked at the night sky. So tired. So cold.

The night had been full of possibilities. Emmett had been full of possibilities.

But none of them would ever come true.

About The Author

Vivian Wolkoff has always been in love with words – even before she could read them. So, it should be no surprise she turned to writing and reading very early in life. She first self-published a poetry book at the age of 13, which received two honorary mentions in contests promoted by a small publishing house in her native Rio de Janeiro, Brazil. Then, she decided to do some living and find out what else she loved. After college and moving cross-continent twice, Vivian decided to turn to self-publishing again. She is the author of *Love You to Death*, a standalone psychological thriller, and the paranormal romance series *Blood Red*.

About The Publisher

Story Shares is a nonprofit focused on supporting the millions of teens and adults who struggle with reading by creating a new shelf in the library specifically for them. The ever-growing collection features content that is compelling and culturally relevant for teens and adults, yet still readable at a range of lower reading levels.

Story Shares generates content by engaging deeply with writers, bringing together a community to create this new kind of book. With more intriguing and approachable stories to choose from, the teens and adults who have fallen behind are improving their skills and beginning to discover the joy of reading. For more information, visit storyshares.org.

Easy to Read. Hard to Put Down.

Out of Time

www.ingramcontent.com/pod-product-compliance
Lightning Source LLC
Chambersburg PA
CBHW051929220626
47052CB00003B/634